DODSWORTH IN PARIS

Written and illustrated by

TIM EGAN

HOUGHTON MIFFLIN COMPANY

BOSTON 2008

To my amazing wife, Ann

www.houghtonmifflinbooks.com

The text of this book is set in Cochin.
The illustrations are ink and watercolor on paper.

Library of Congress Cataloging-in-Publication Number 2007047732

ISBN-13: 978-0-618-98062-8

Printed in Singapore
TWP 10 9 8 7 6 5 4 3 2 1

CONTENTS

CHAPTER ONE

BONJOUR

The ship sailed into Paris.

Dodsworth was very excited.

So was the duck.

They had never been to France before.

“Now, I have one rule,” said Dodsworth.
“You can’t cause any trouble here.”
“I wouldn’t dream of it,” said the duck.
Dodsworth just looked at him.

The streets were full of life.
There were jugglers and dancers
and painters everywhere.
One painter had a beret on his head.
The duck liked the beret.

The duck picked up an acorn cap.

He put it on his head.

It looked like a beret, sort of.

"Very debonair," said Dodsworth.

They sat down for lunch at a café.

"Bonjour," said the waiter.

"That means 'Hello,'" Dodsworth told the duck.

"Oh, well then, 'banjo' to you, too," said the duck.

The duck looked at the menu.
It was all in French, so he couldn't read any of it.
"How do you say, 'macaroni'?" he asked.
"Just like that, *monsieur,*" said the waiter.
The duck smiled.

A mime performed on the sidewalk as they ate.

When they finished, Dodsworth paid the waiter.

"This is the wrong kind of money, *monsieur*," said the waiter. "You must change it into euros at the bank."

There was a bank across the street.
"Okay," said Dodsworth to the duck,
"you stay here and don't move, like him."
He pointed to the mime.

The mime was perfectly still, like a statue.
"I can do that," said the duck.
He jumped up on the table and
stayed perfectly still as well.
Some folks tossed coins at the mime.
Some tossed a few coins at the duck.

Dodsworth returned and they checked in to a hotel, the Chateau de Paris. From their room they could see the Eiffel Tower.

"This trip is off to a great start," said Dodsworth.

CHAPTER TWO
THE CITY OF LIGHTS

The duck woke up early to the sound of bells.

The sound rang all across Paris.

The duck loved bells.

They were coming from Notre Dame Cathedral.

The duck looked over at Dodsworth.

He was snoring.

The duck didn't want to wake him.

He quietly climbed out the window.

The duck walked over to the cathedral.
He climbed all the way up to the bell tower.
There was a bent-over fellow ringing the bells.
“Can I try?” asked the duck.

“Sure,” said the fellow. “I could use a break.”

He held out a rope for the duck.

The duck pulled with all his might.

The bells echoed over the city.

Dodsworth woke up.

He saw the duck was missing.

"Oh no," he said.

He looked out the window.

He called for the duck.

"Morning!" yelled the duck from the cathedral. "I got to ring the bells!"

Dodsworth laughed a little, but shouted, "You can't just leave like that! Do you understand?"

The duck nodded and waved.

Dodsworth rented a bicycle.

The duck sat in the basket.

They rode over to the Eiffel Tower.

“Now promise me,” said Dodsworth,

“you won’t leave my side.”

“Duck’s honor,” said the duck.

They went to the top of the Eiffel Tower.
They could see for miles.
"Wow," said a lady nearby. "Imagine
how far a paper airplane would fly from
here."

The duck loved the idea.

He opened Dodsworth's backpack.

He took out some paper.

He made airplane after airplane.

Some flew better than others.

All the while, Dodsworth was enjoying the view.

He heard excitement from the crowd below.

"Something's going on down there," he said.

He looked over at the duck.

Dodsworth screamed.

"What are you doing?" shouted
Dodsworth. "That's our money!"
The duck was making the airplanes
out of euros.
He didn't realize it was money.
"Oops," said the duck.

"Oh, this is just perfect!" yelled Dodsworth.

"We've been here for two days and now we're almost out of money. Well done, duck."

CHAPTER THREE

AN AFTERNOON RIDE

Dodsworth and the duck pedaled down the street.
Dodsworth was very angry.
He scowled at the duck.
A tear fell onto the duck's beak.

Dodsworth felt bad that he had yelled at him.

"Oh, it's okay," he said. "Everyone makes mistakes. Don't cry."

The duck smiled.

He wasn't really crying.

He just had something in his eye for a second.

“We could use a bit more money, though,” said Dodsworth.

Just then, they saw a sign in a bakery window. It said BREAD DELIVERY JOB.

“Well, there we have it,” said Dodsworth.

They went inside and got the job.

Moments later, they were riding all around Paris, delivering bread.
They rode over the Seine River and along the beautiful cobblestone streets of the great city.
Dodsworth and the duck were never happier.

They turned a corner and rode over a hill.
Many folks were cheering on the sidewalks.
They cheered and cheered as Dodsworth
and the duck rode by.
"It's such a friendly place," said Dodsworth.

Suddenly, another bicycle came speeding by.
"Whoa!" said the duck. "What was that?"
Then another bicycle raced by, then another.

Soon, hundreds of bicycles were all
around.
They were in the Tour de France!
Dodsworth pedaled as fast as he could.
The duck held on to his acorn cap.

They came to a turn.

Dodsworth tried to steer as best he could.

It wasn't quite good enough.

Their bicycle crashed into a hedge of bushes.

Bread went flying everywhere.

Dodsworth was okay but the duck wasn't moving.

"Duck?" said Dodsworth. "Are you all right?"

The duck just lay there.

"Oh no," said Dodsworth. "Please. Speak to me."

The duck opened one eye.

"*Bonjour,*" he said.

Dodsworth hugged the duck.

The duck didn't really like to be hugged.

CHAPTER FOUR

A LASTING IMPRESSION

They lost their delivery job.
They had to return the bicycle.
Since they didn't have much money left,
they sat in the park and tried to think
of ways to make more.

A crowd started walking by.
"Pardon me," said Dodsworth to a lady.
"Where is everyone going?"
"Why, to the Louvre, of course," said the lady.
"It's free today."

Anything free sounded good, so they followed
the crowd to the great Louvre Museum.
Dodsworth stared at the Mona Lisa.
The Mona Lisa stared back.
"That's it!" shouted Dodsworth.
He grabbed the duck and ran out of the
museum.

"I love painting!" said Dodsworth. "I'll make a picture and we'll sell it. How tough could that be?"

"Could be pretty tough," said the duck.

Dodsworth took out some brushes and paint.

He spent the day making a picture of Paris.

The painting came out beautiful.

The duck was impressed.

They took the painting around to galleries.

Every one said the same thing: *"Non."*

"They just don't know what's good," said the duck.

Dodsworth was sad.

As the lights of the park twinkled that evening, he fell asleep on a bench.

The duck did not like his friend to be sad.

He had an idea.

He stood perfectly still like a statue again.
He waited for folks to throw coins.
He stood like that for almost two hours.
Nobody threw any coins.
They didn't even seem to notice.
They were too busy watching a group
of dancers.

"Okay," said the duck, "if it's dancing you want, it's dancing you'll get."

He started dancing like a maniac.

He was not a good dancer.

Instead of tossing money, folks just laughed.

The duck fell asleep next to Dodsworth.

The night was cold and drizzly.

It wasn't a good night's sleep.

When they woke up in the morning,
Dodsworth said, “Oh no! What happened?”
His painting was all blurry.
There was paint on the duck’s feet.
He had danced on the painting by mistake.

A fellow came walking by.

"Magnifique!" he shouted.

"It is a great impression of Paris,

a brilliant use of color and light.

I will give you one hundred euros for it."

Dodsworth and the duck were thrilled.

They went and had a splendid breakfast.
Giant hot air balloons started floating overhead.
"Now, that looks like a fun way to celebrate," said Dodsworth.
The duck agreed.

They went to the hot air balloon field.
They climbed in a balloon and were soon sailing over Paris.
As the wind changed, and as the balloon started floating away toward England, Dodsworth and the duck said *"Au revoir"* and toasted to the City of Lights.